Roars from readers about

"*Every* kid (and grown-up) will identify with this book."

"A fun story with a simple, educational twist - working with others to solve problems. "

"This book makes me want to sit by a river, listen to the wind and throw rocks into the river."

"Learning how to be a friend is like learning how to read and count - the lessons must start early in life. Thanks to this book, and other books by Miss Nemec, our children can develop a love for learning."

You can write your review on line, too!

EDITED BY
Paige Ireland
Patricia C. Pyle
Teresa Wood

ISBN: 978-1-947608-02-3

Nemec Productions, LLC Alexandria, VA, USA

This is my book

_____

Today's date

_____

This book is from

_____

Draw a picture here!

This book is dedicated to:
my darling brother
Jimmy/James/Jim Nemec JR/III
1953—2011

****

And to

Margie Huge Zylich,
who is beating cancer while remaining a positive, encouraging, life-long friend to everyone she knows. She tells me that I am smart and beautiful and glitzy, and I tell her that she is, too -- because she is!

Margie, my prayers are with you.
Full Site: http://www.caringbridge.org/visit/margeryezylich
Mobile: http://m.caringbridge.org/visit/margeryezylich

Throwing Rocks in the River

Written and Illustrated
By
Gale Nemec

One beautiful summer day, Jeremy had a big fight with his mother.

He was so angry that he stormed out of the house, slammed the door and stomped down to the river.

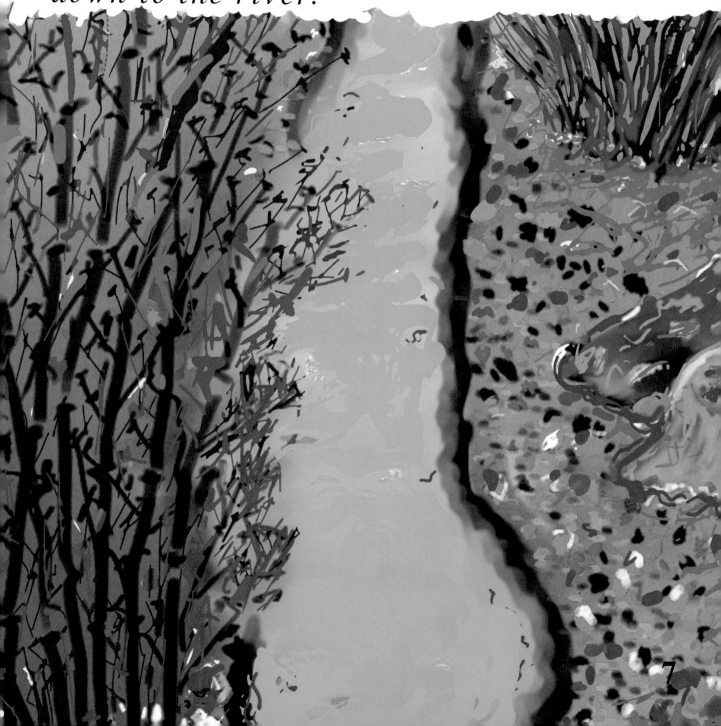

When he reached the river, he saw his best friend Jessica. She was throwing rocks in the river.

Each time a rock landed in the river it made a "plunk" sound.

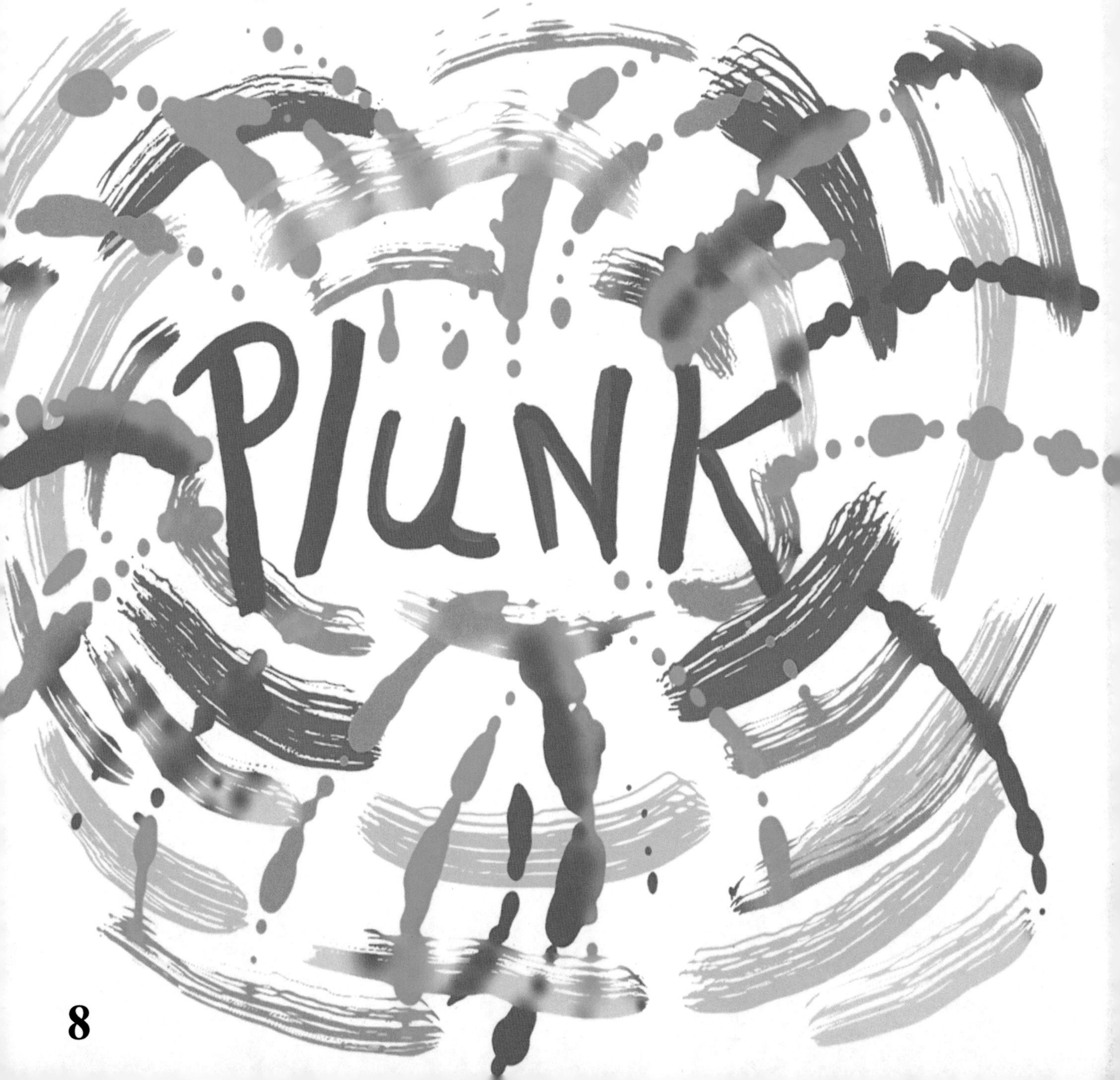
PLUNK

Jeremy sat down next to Jessica and threw ten rocks into the river, one rock at a time.

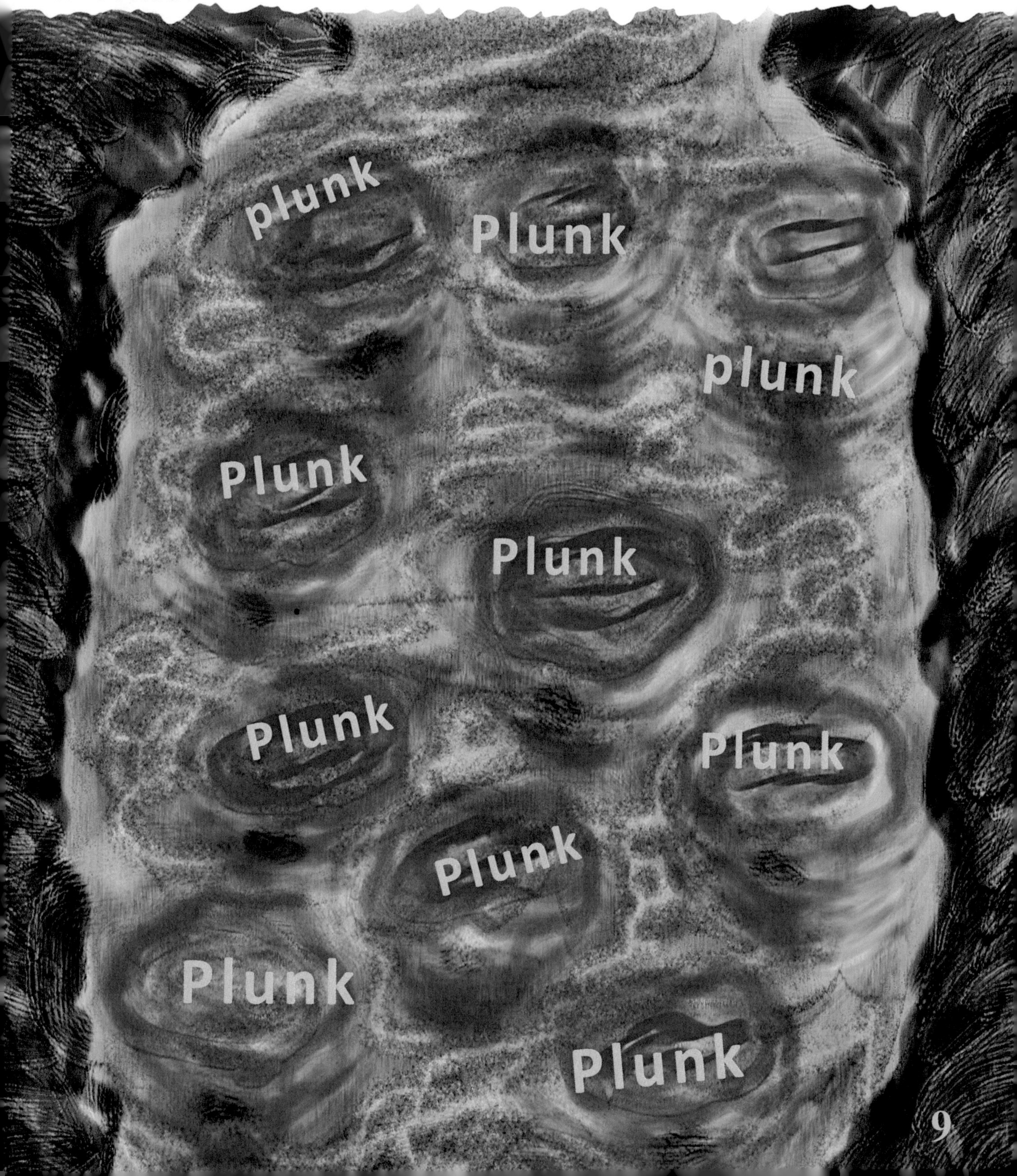
plunk
Plunk
plunk
Plunk
Plunk
Plunk
Plunk
Plunk
Plunk
Plunk

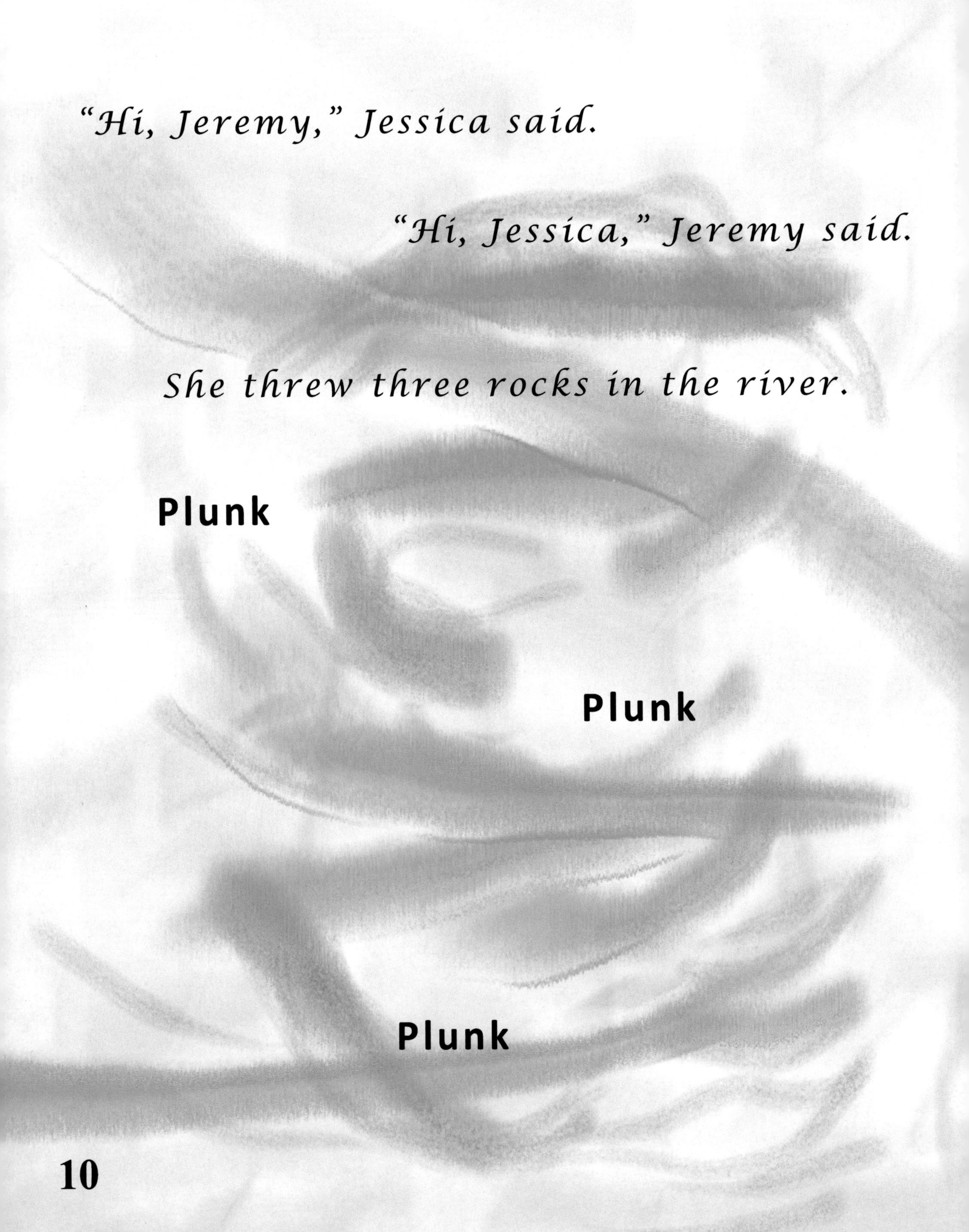

"Hi, Jeremy," Jessica said.

"Hi, Jessica," Jeremy said.

She threw three rocks in the river.

Plunk

Plunk

Plunk

After a while, Jeremy asked, "Jessica, why are you throwing rocks into the river?" And then he threw five rocks into the river.

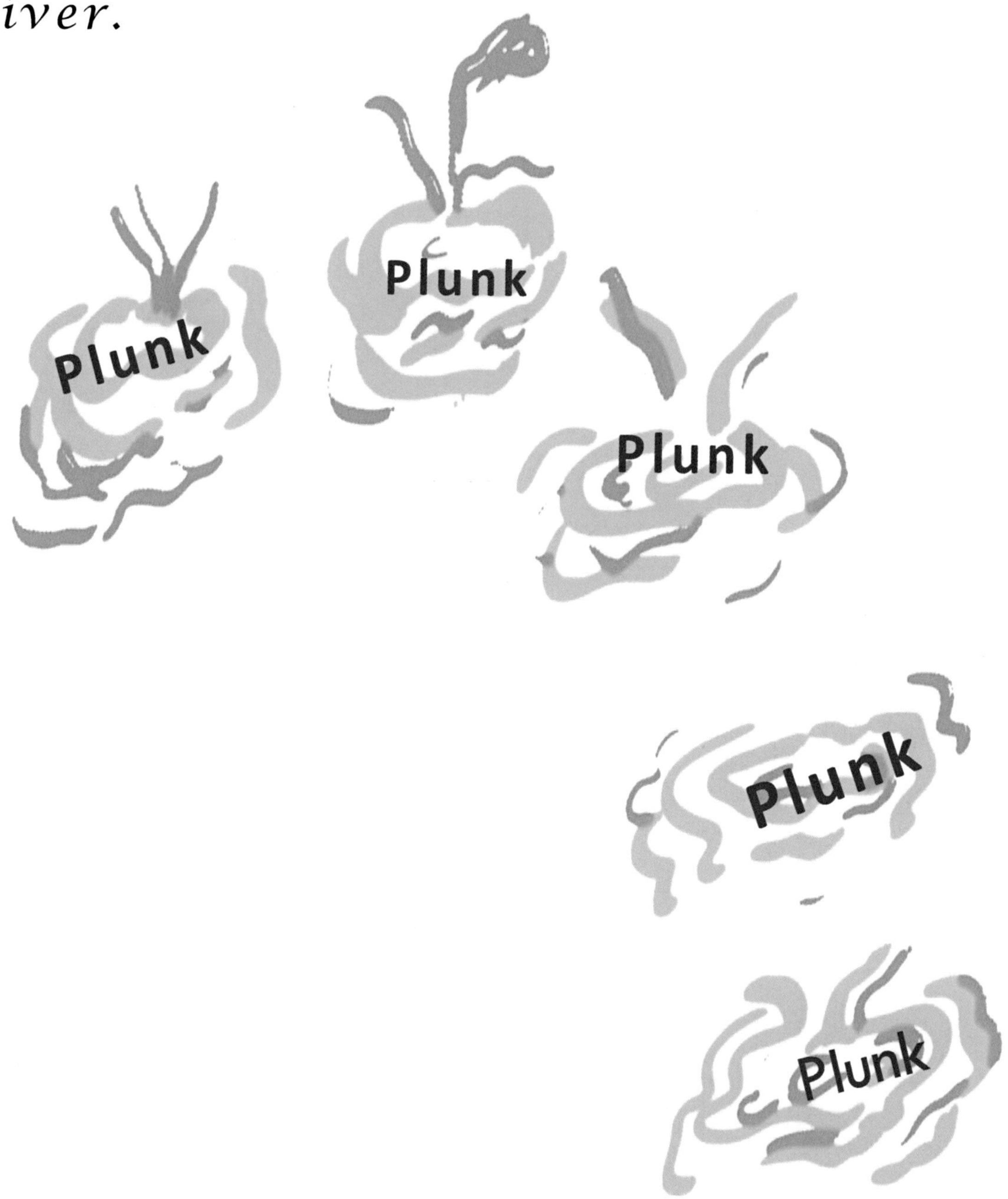
Plunk
Plunk
Plunk
Plunk
Plunk

Because," she groaned, "I had a big fight with my Dad." And she threw seven rocks into the river.

Plunk
Plunk
Plunk
Plunk
Plunk
Plunk
Plunk

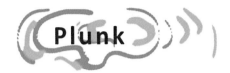

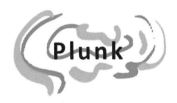

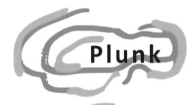

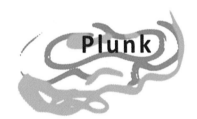

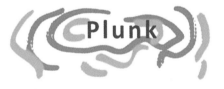

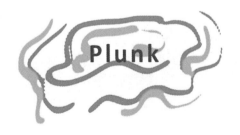

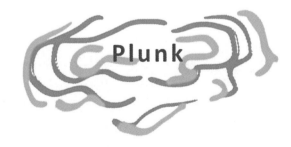

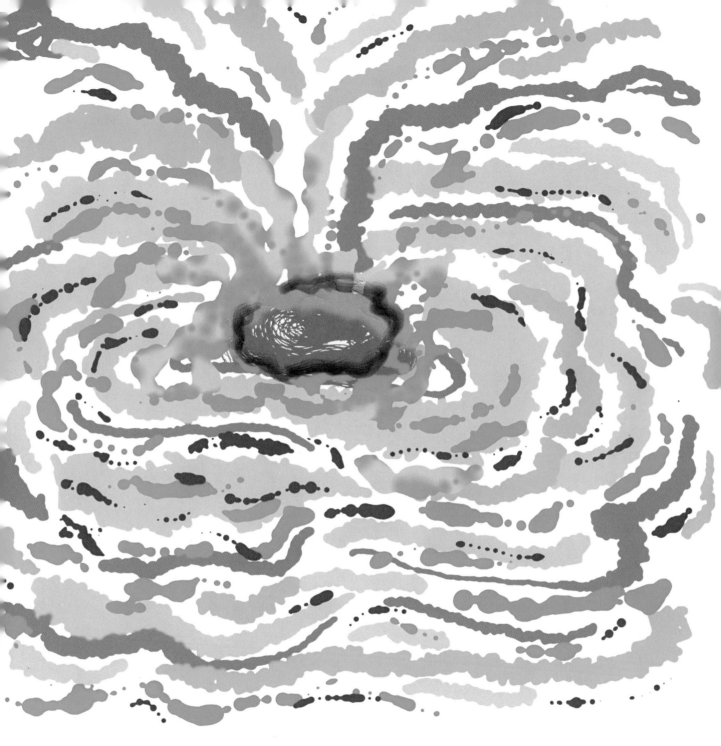

Time passed and Jessica asked, "Jeremy, why are *you* throwing rocks into the river?" And she threw *one* big rock into the river.

"Because," he sighed, "I had a big fight with my Mom!" And he hurled seven rocks into the river!

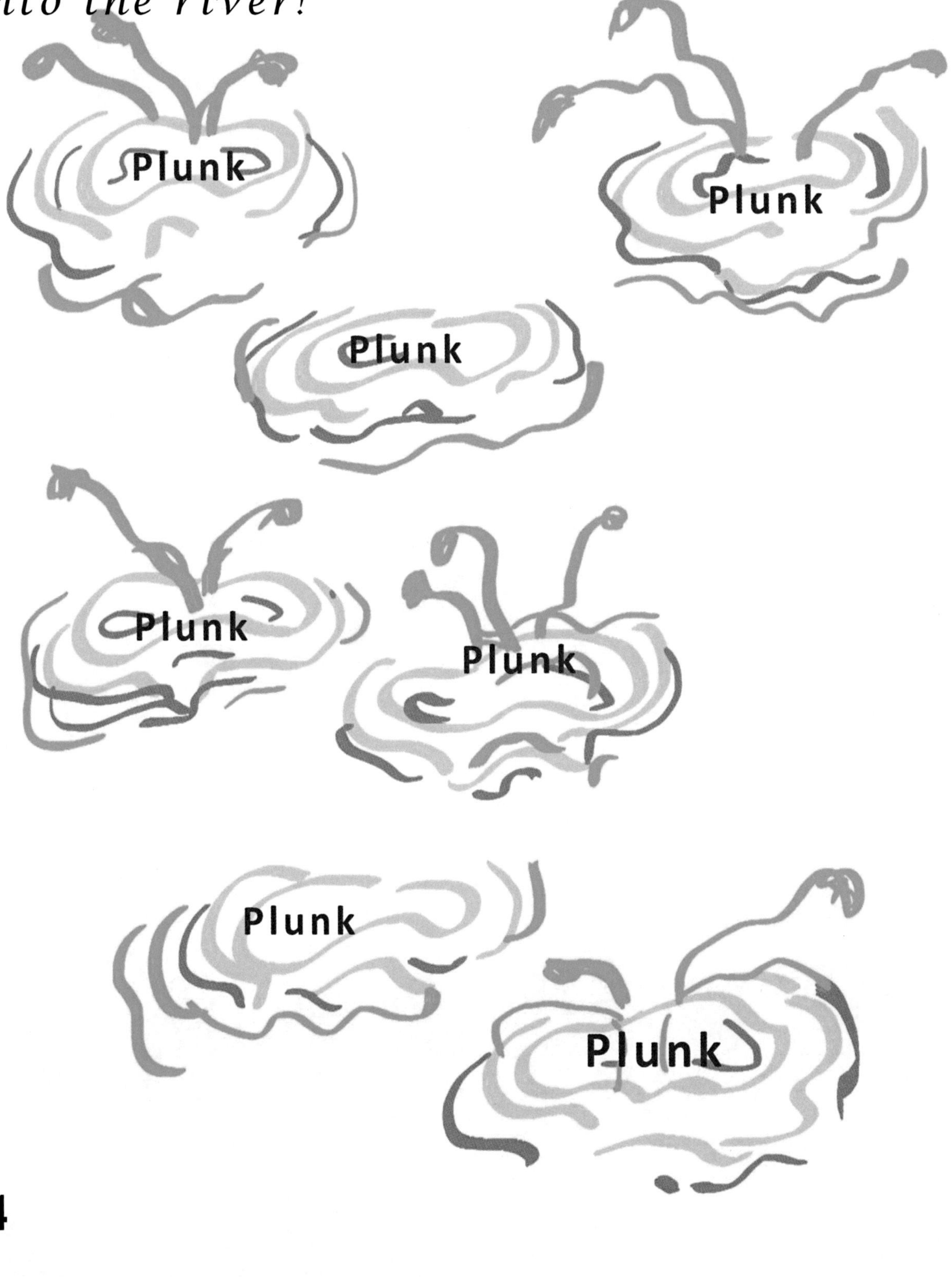
Plunk
Plunk
Plunk
Plunk
Plunk
Plunk
Plunk

"What did you argue about?" asked Jessica.

For a very long time there was almost complete silence as the two friends sat side by side, listened to the wind in the trees, picked up rocks, and threw them into the river.

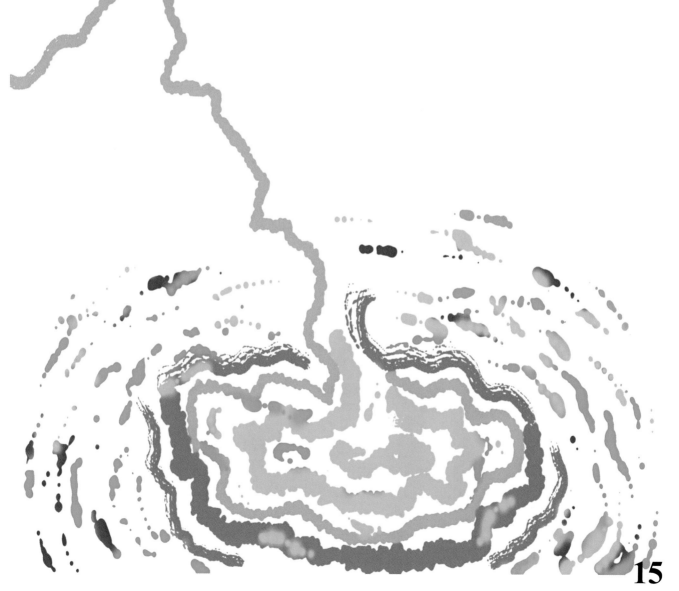

"I wanted a grilled cheese sandwich for lunch. But nooooo! Mom made me a peanut butter and jelly sandwich!" he protested as he threw eight rocks into the river.

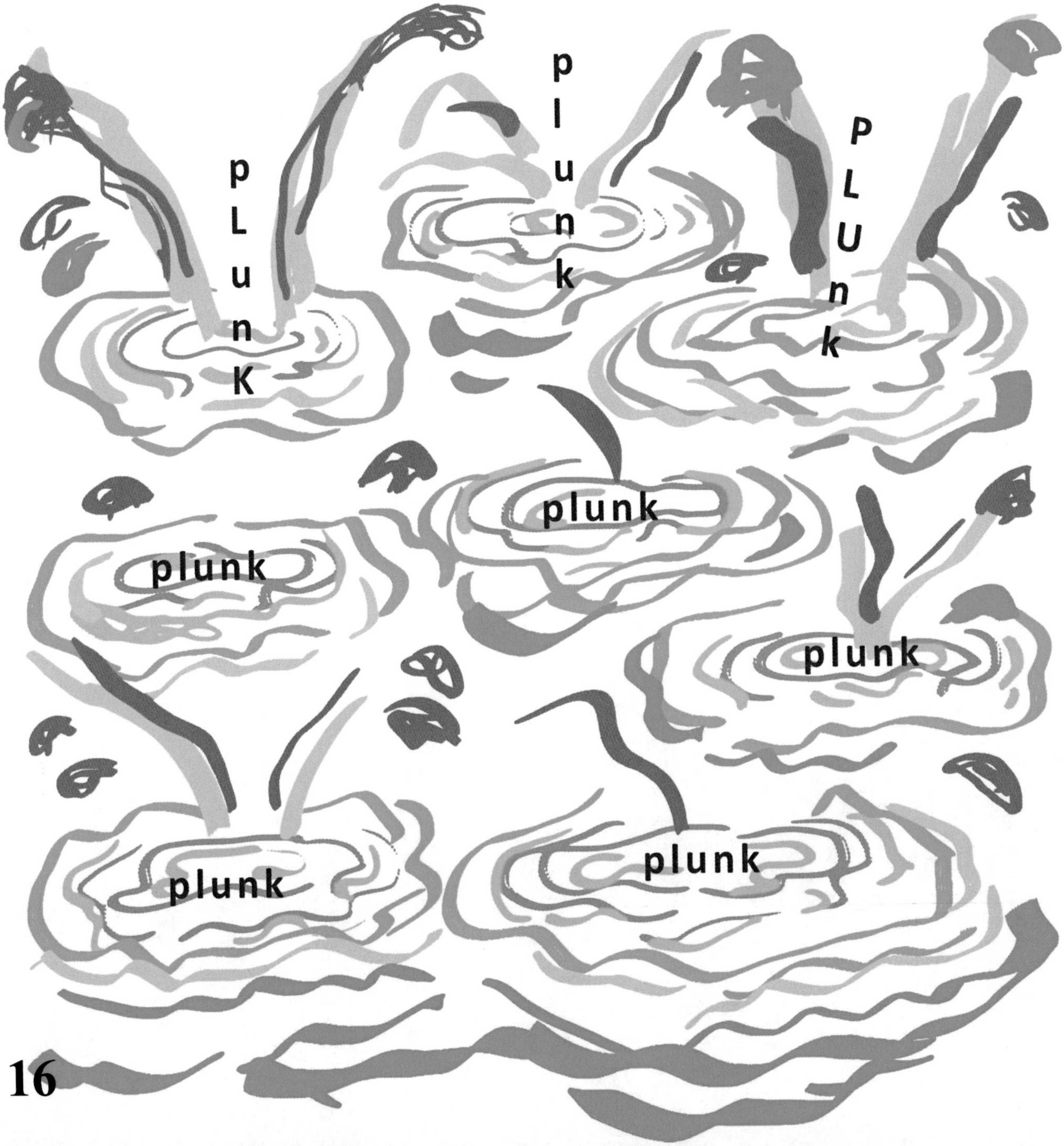

pLunK
plunk
PLUnk
plunk
plunk
plunk
plunk
plunk

"Gee. That's really amazing!" replied Jessica.

"Why is that so amazing? Mom would not give me what I wanted to eat! She gave me what *she* wanted me to eat!" shouted Jeremy. "Hey! Are you taking sides with my Mom??"

"NO!" exclaimed Jessica.

"Then what do you mean?" bellowed Jeremy.

"I wanted a peanut butter and jelly sandwich and dad made *me a grilled cheese sandwich!*" Jessica shouted back.

She hurled ten rocks into the river!

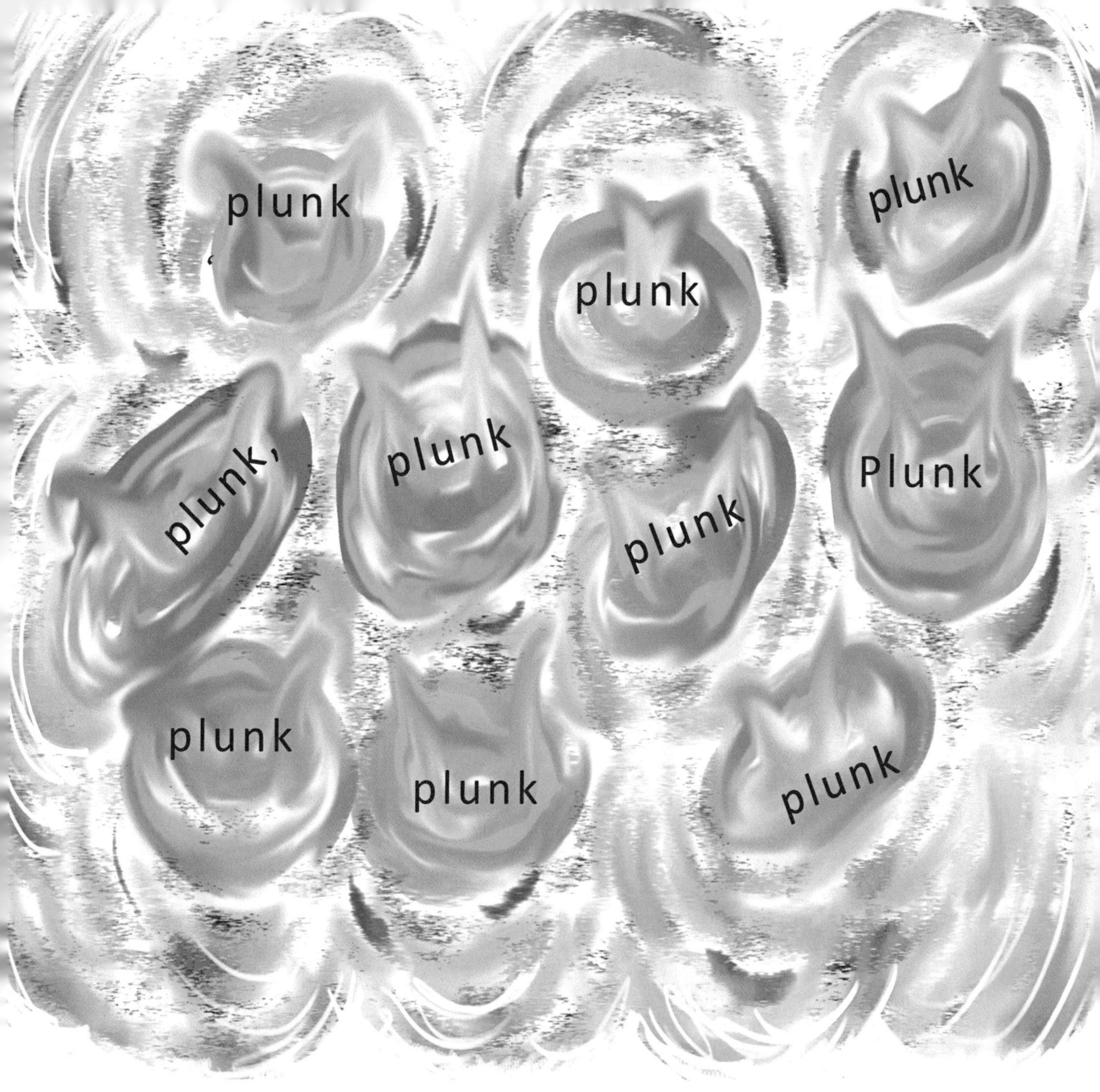
plunk
plunk
plunk
plunk,
plunk
plunk
Plunk
plunk
plunk
plunk

"Oh," was all Jeremy could say.

The two friends stared at each other in disbelief. Each parent made what the other friend wanted for lunch!

Then. . .

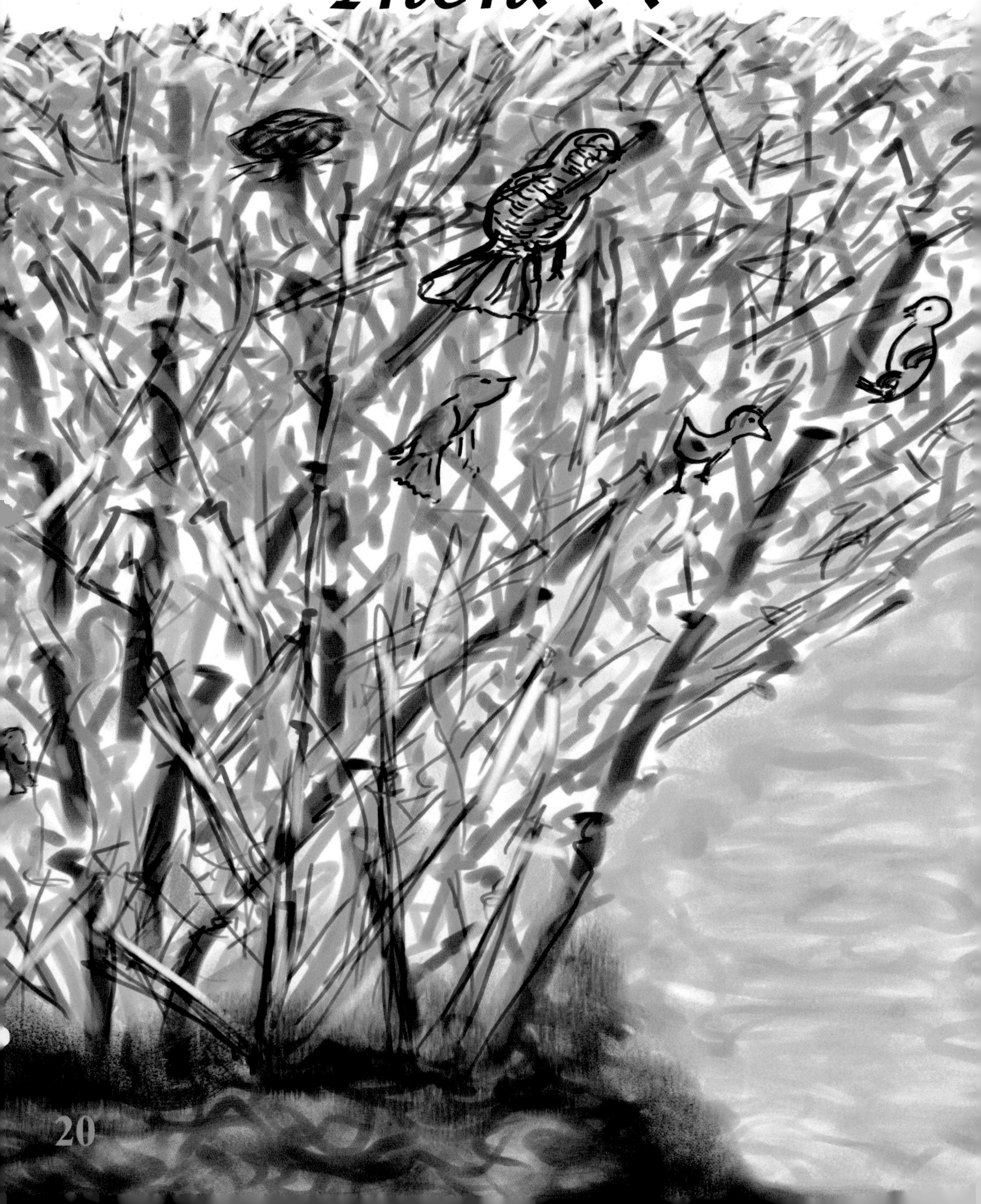

Both of their empty stomachs began to growl and then to grumble!

The grumbling sounded like bears growling a greeting and tigers on the prowl.

Growl . . .

    Grumble. . .

    Grrrowwlllllll. . .

Grrrruuummmblllleeee. . .

Grrrrrrrrooooowwwwllllll. . .

Grrrumblllleee. . .

    Gggrrrrroowlll. . .

Then it sounded like a drum-roll on huge kettle drums playing in an orchestra in a gigantic concert hall!

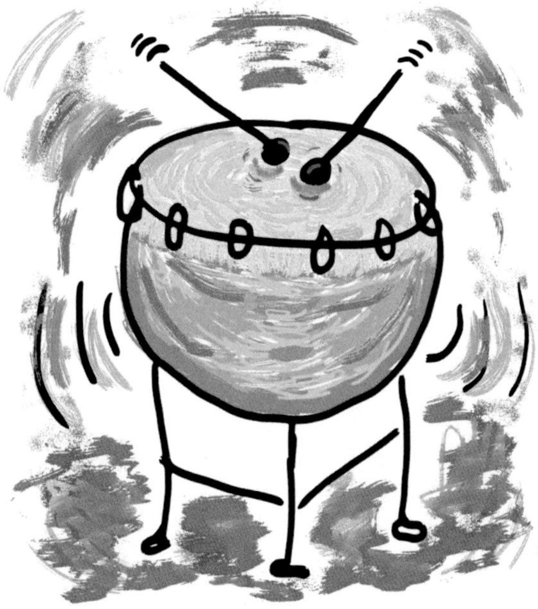

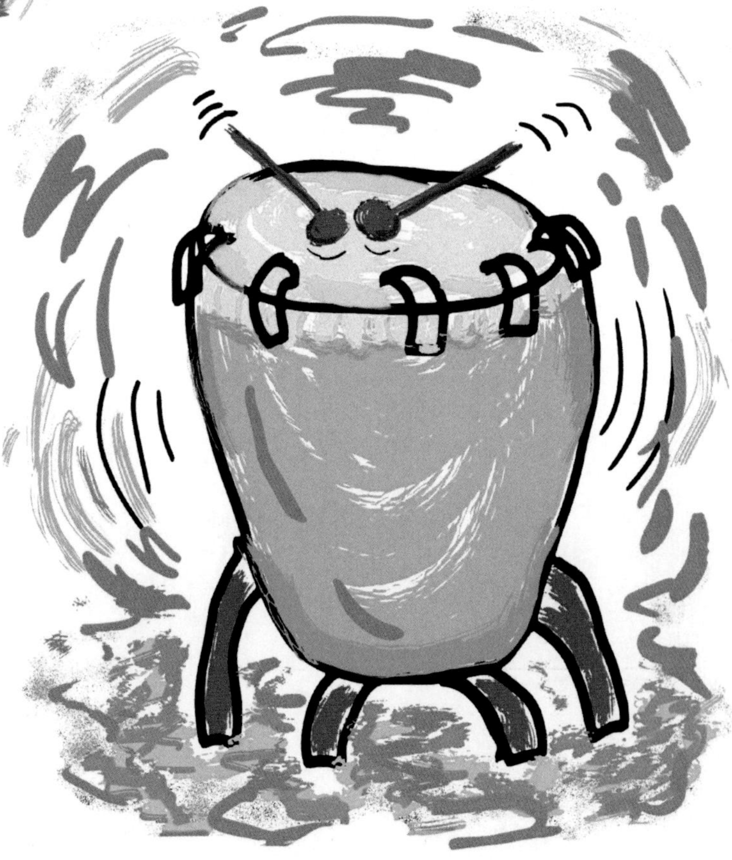

Hearing each other's stomachs, Jeremy started to snicker and Jessica started to giggle.

Then they both began to chuckle. Then they both started to chortle. Then they both erupted into enormous peals of laughter!!

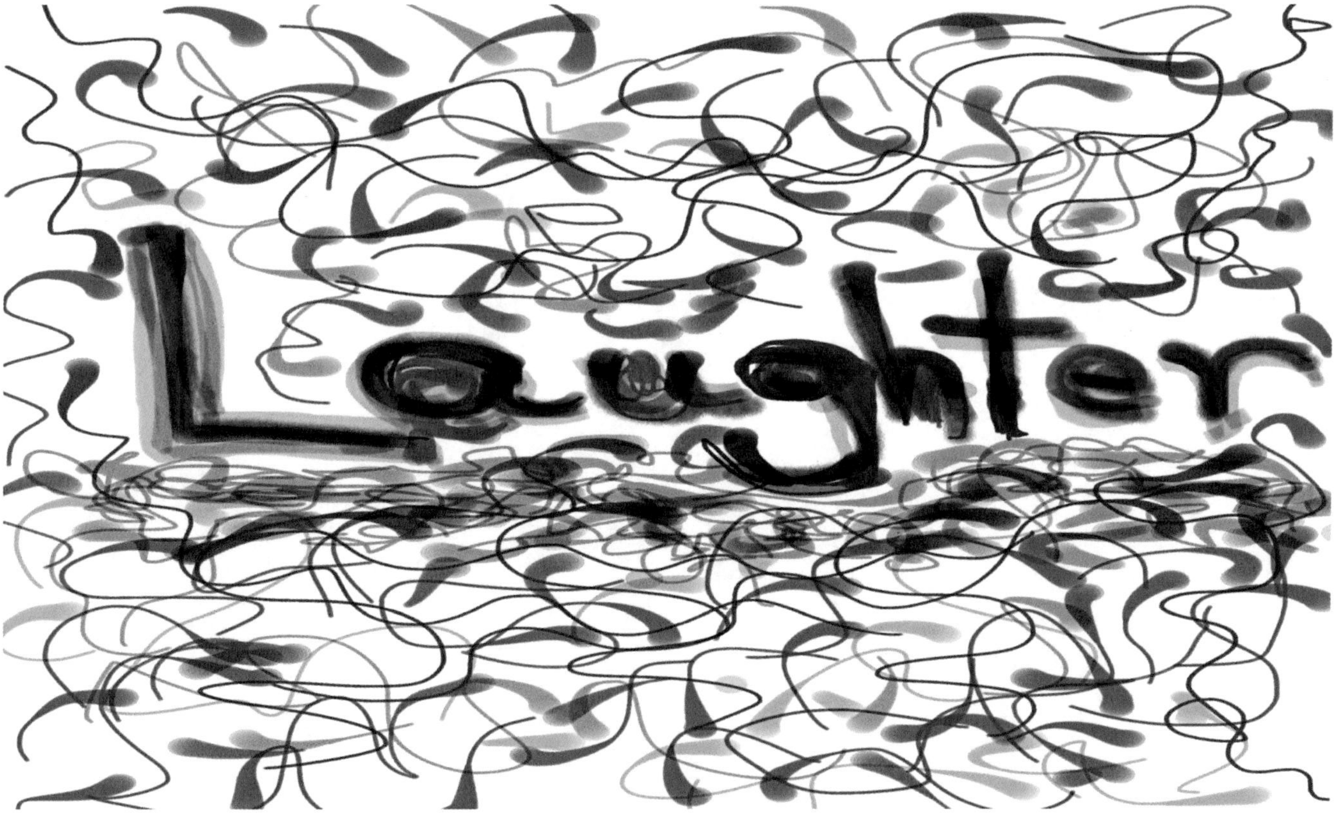
Laughter

They laughed so hard that they guffawed, which means they were laughing really, really hard!

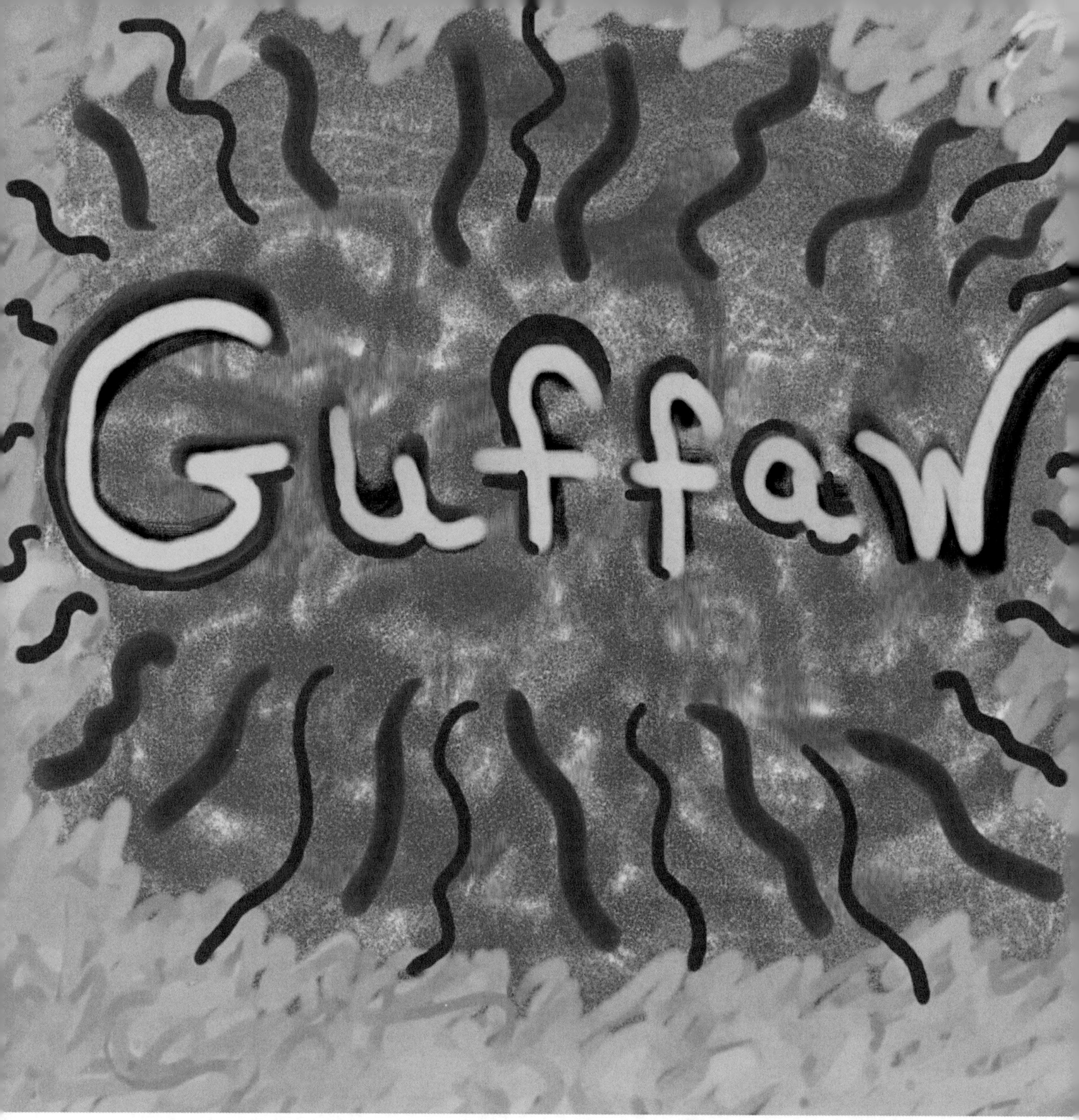
Guffaw

They guffawed so much that they both fell back and rolled around on the ground!!

After several l-o-n-g minutes, their laughter changed from guffaws to snorts to snickers and then to twitters.

Snickering, Jessica said, "Okay. Because we didn't want to eat what our parents made us for lunch, we are both hungry and that's a problem!"

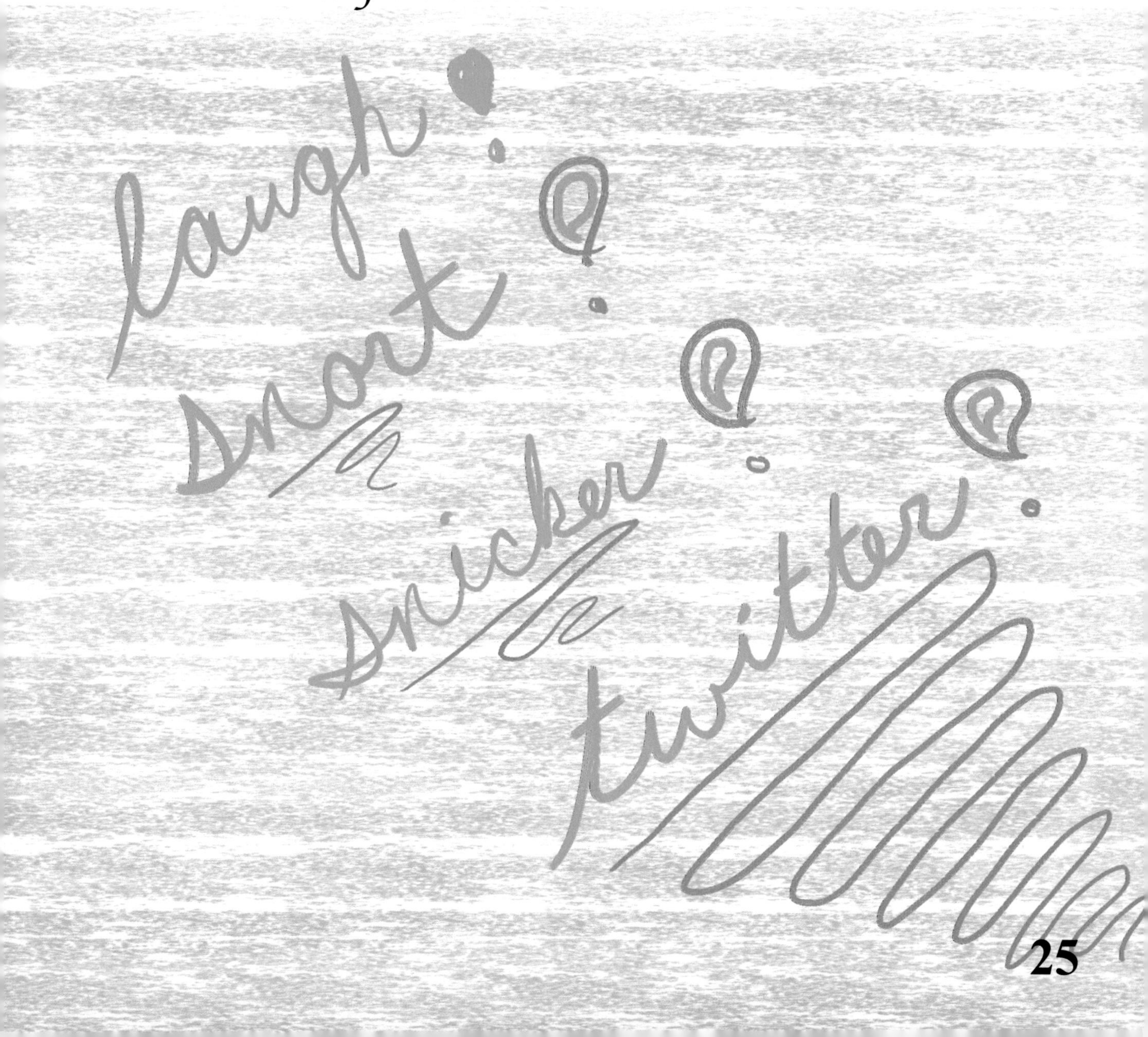
laugh!
snort!
snicker!
twitter!

"What's really silly is that we both like what our parents fixed for us, but we didn't want to eat it today, and that's really selfish! Now, what are we going to do?"

"Hummm," Jessica thought out loud. "I have an idea!" and she grinned.

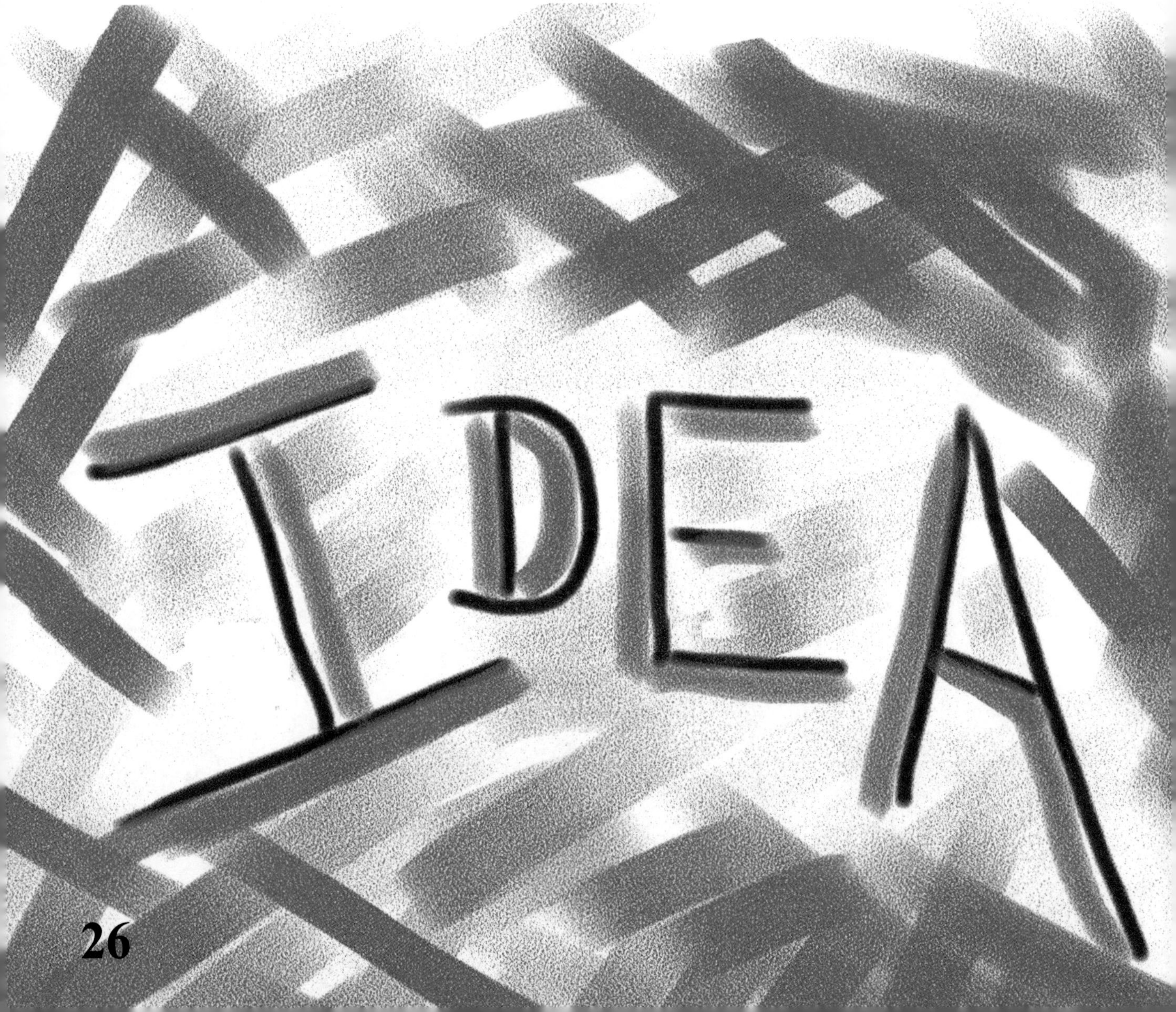
IDEA

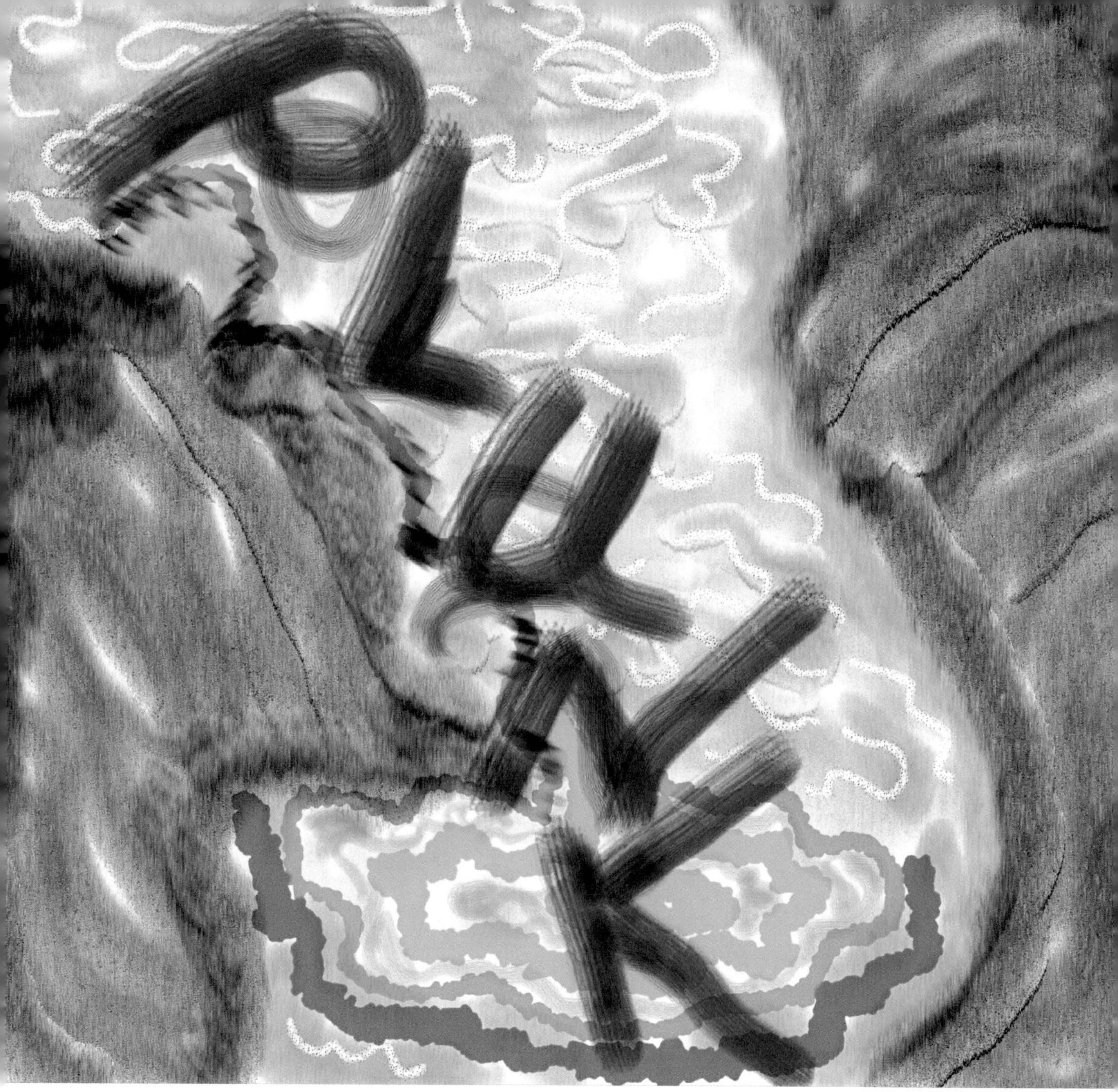
PLUNK

"What??" smiled Jeremy as he picked up a rock and threw it into the river.

But the rock hit the river bank and tumbled down.

Jessica hurriedly said, "*You* go to *your* house and get the peanut butter and jelly sandwich and. . ."

". . .you go to *your* house and get the grilled cheese sandwich!" Jeremy excitedly interrupted.

At the exact same time they said, "We'll bring the sandwiches back here and have a picnic lunch!"

"*SUPER IDEA!*" they both hollered at the same time.

The best friends looked at each other and realized they had solved a problem.

By working together they were both going to eat what they wanted to eat for lunch.

They were so excited! They looked at each other and said, "We should apologize to our parents, too."

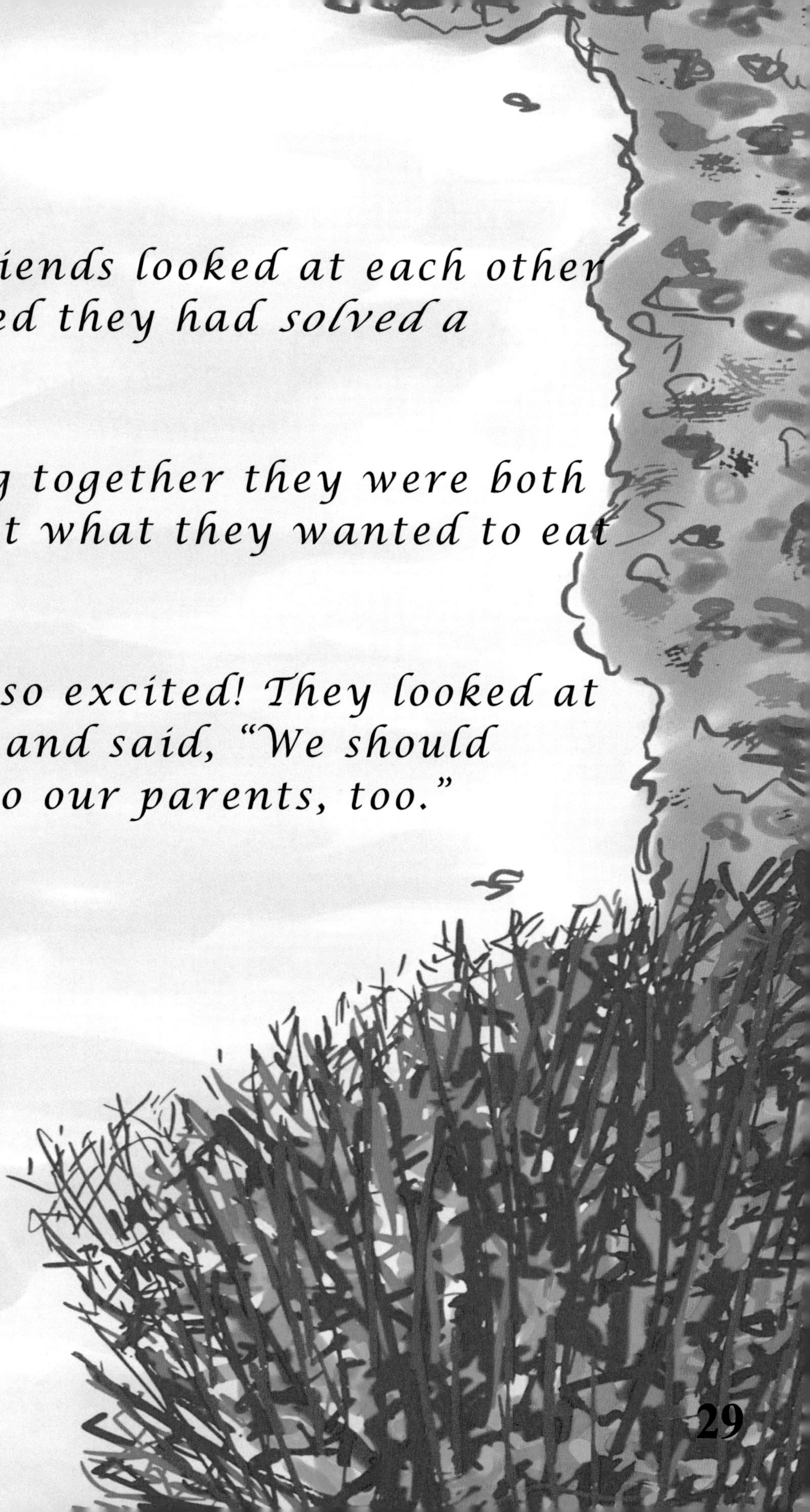

"Yes," they agreed, "That would be another good idea. We were both rude."

So the best friends went to their homes, apologized to their parents for their behavior, and got their lunch.

I'M SORRY MOM...
I'M SORRY DAD...

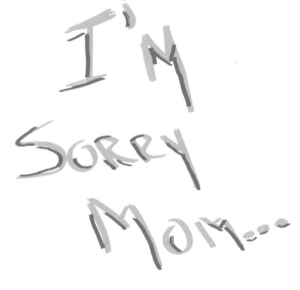

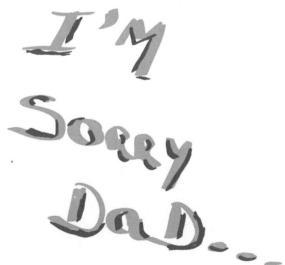

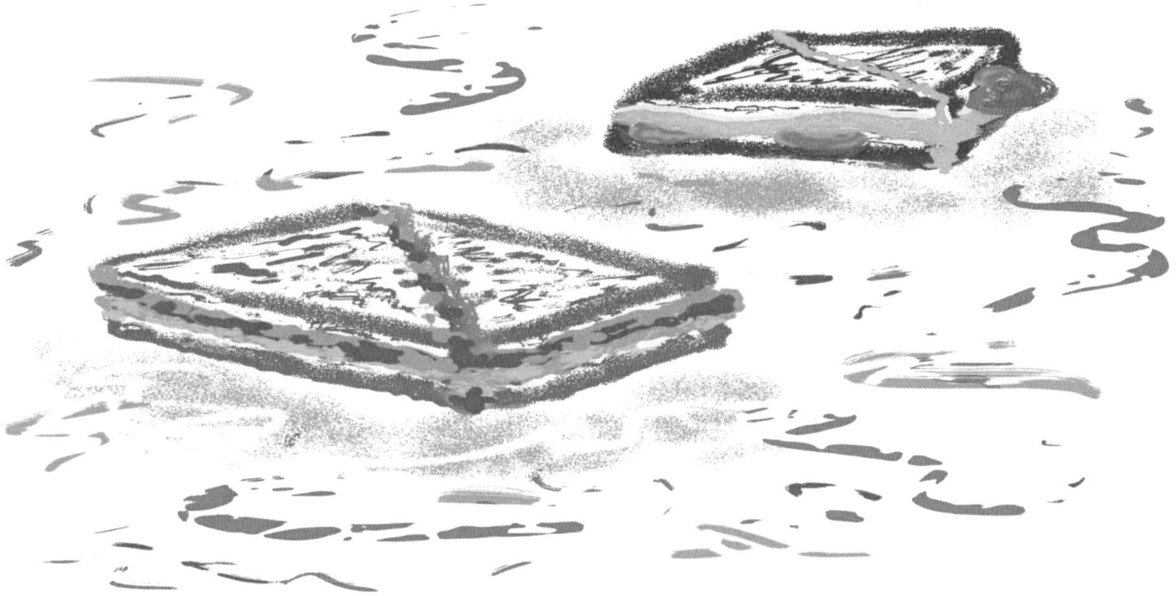

Their parents gave them their sandwiches, carrot and celery sticks, milk, an orange and an apple for dessert, and paper towels to use as napkins. It was the perfect lunch.

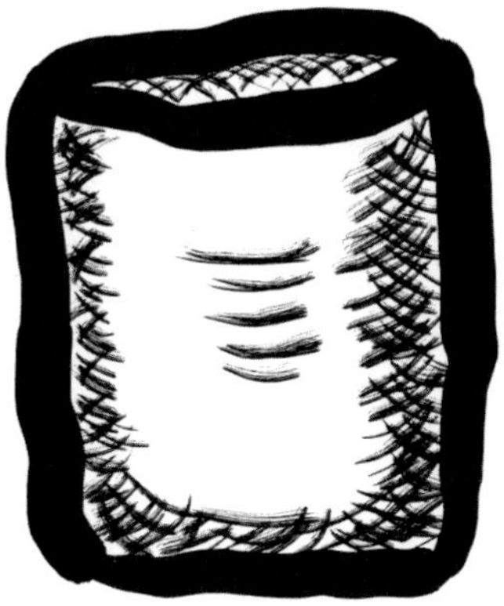

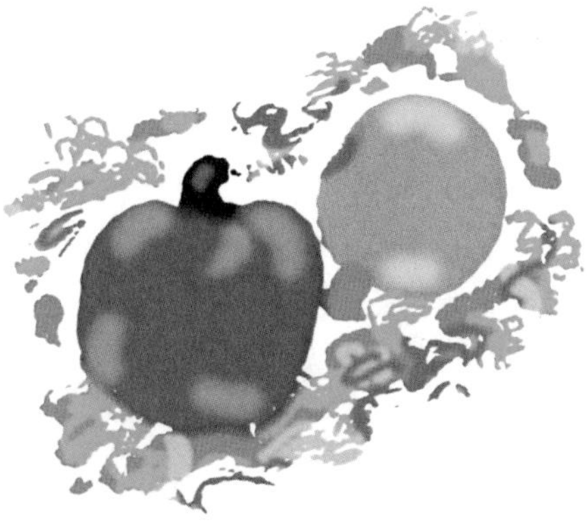

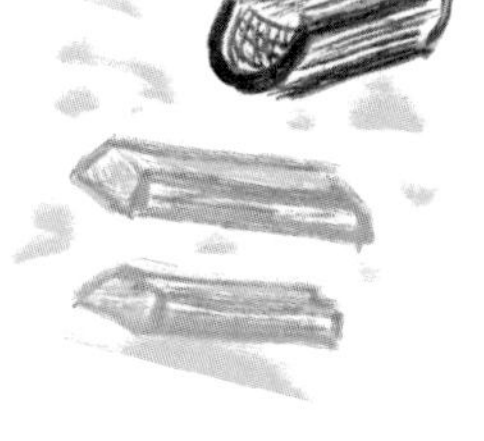

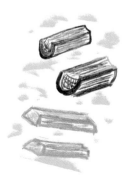

Jessica and Jeremy sat on two huge rocks and enjoyed a picnic in the warm summer sun.

Jessica ate the peanut butter and jelly sandwich, and Jeremy ate the grilled cheese sandwich with pickles!!

Gee whiz they were happy!

It was a nice day, there were plenty of rocks to throw in the river, and they had good food to eat.

They talked about what had happened and started to giggle . . .

. . . which led to a chortle. . .

. . . which led to a howl.

They hooted and hollered and roared so much that milk came out of both of their noses!!

"Disgusting!" they roared at the same.

Laughing, they said to each other, "This is a good day."

Even though the day had started out with both friends having fights with their parents, together Jessica and Jeremy solved their problems.

Which led to a good day, which led to a summer picnic, which led to. . .

. . . guess what it led to??

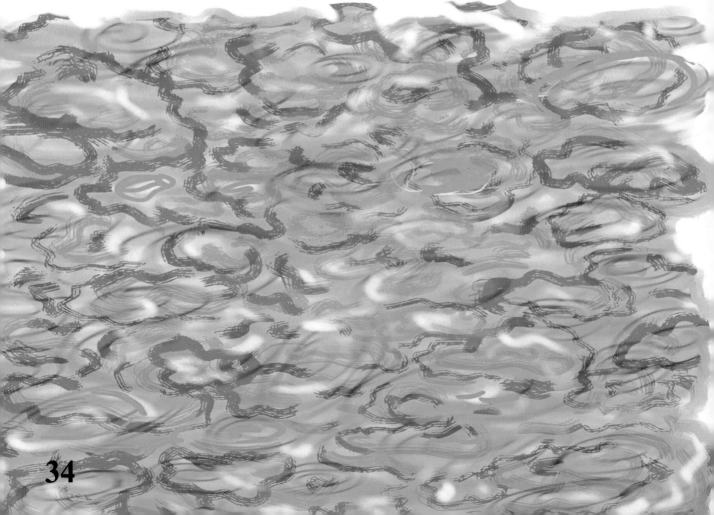

You guessed it! Throwing rocks in the river. One rock after the other,
after the other,
after the other.

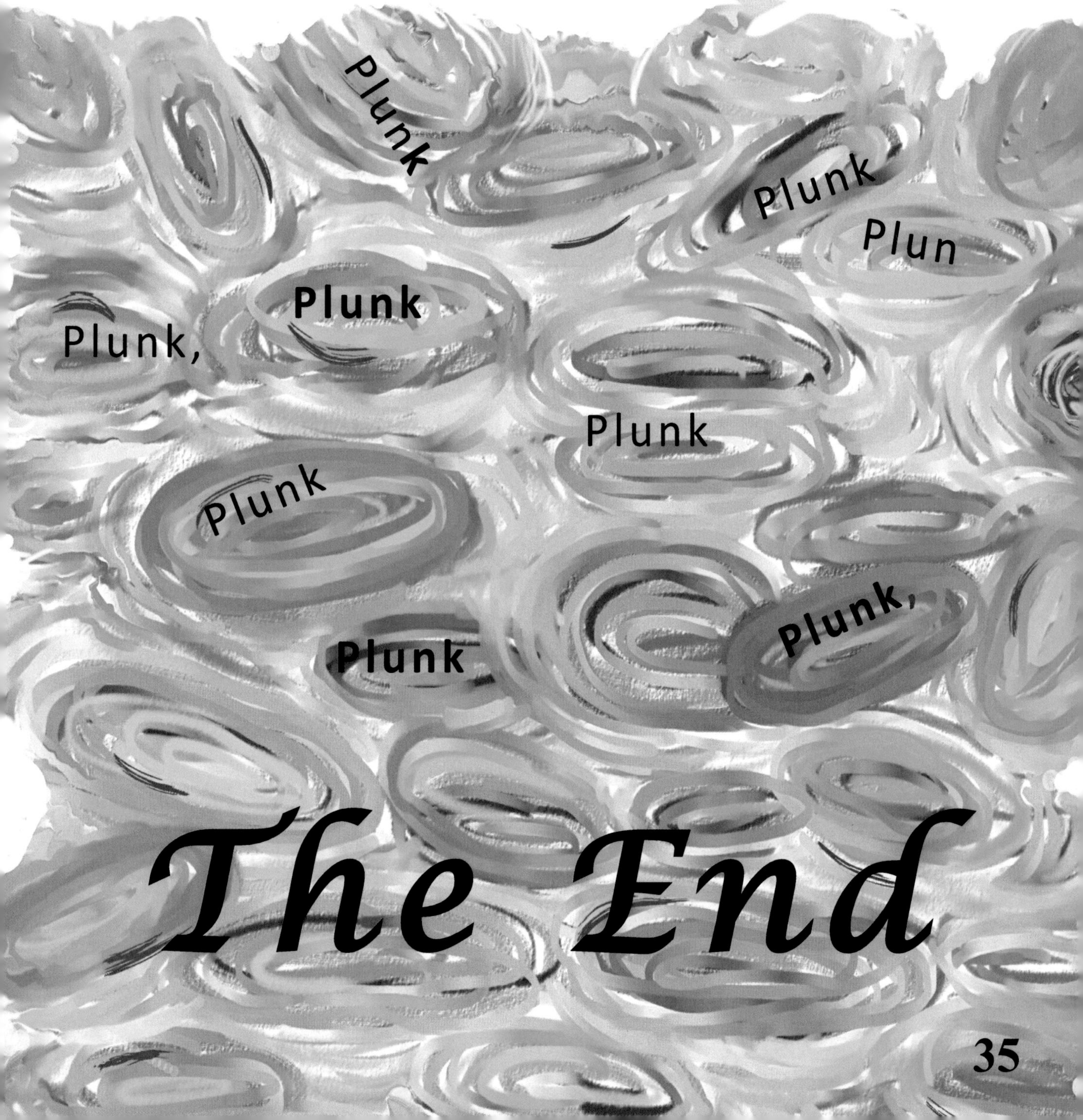
Plunk
Plunk
Plun
Plunk
Plunk,
Plunk
Plunk
Plunk
Plunk,

The End

Hello Reader!

Did you know there are many different ways to say the word "*laugh*"? Some of the words are guffaw, chortle, snicker, twitter, hoot and holler, roar and chuckle.

When you read the story again, look for those words.

Find the word "*plunk*" and discover how many rocks Jessica and Jeremy threw into the river.

How many birds can you find on page twenty?

Send Mizz Nemec an
email and tell her how
you solved a problem.
Did you solve it alone?
Were you with another
person or were you with
a team?

www.GaleNemecBooks.com

GaleNemecBooks@gmail.com

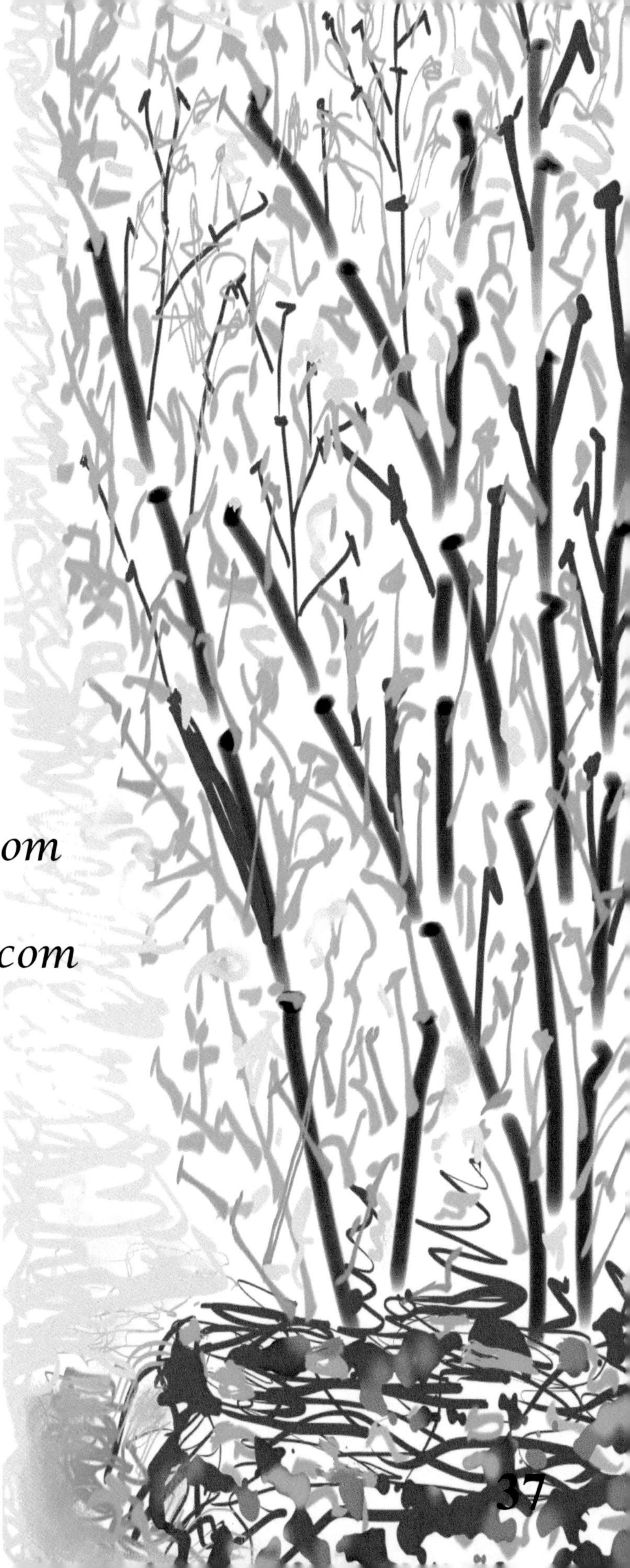

BOOKS and E-BOOKS BY GALE NEMEC
Ask your local bookstore for Gale's books
Visit www.GaleNemecBooks.com.

FICTION
There's a Bear on a Bench
The Great Elephant Rescue
Throwing Rocks in the River
Trevor and the T's
Dragon in the Mirror - a rhyming coloring book
Little Stockey & The Miracle of Christmas
Hugging God
Hugging Jesus
Andy's Adventurous Nightmare
Hugs - a quiet-time coloring book
Valentine Cards for the Christian Faith
Valentine Cards for Valentine's Day

BILINGUAL: SPANISH AND ENGLISH
Hay un Oso en la Banca (There's a Bear on a Bench)

SPANISH
El pequeño Stockey y el Milagro de la Navidad
(Little Stockey & the Miracle of Christmas)

INTERACTIVE BOOKS ON YOUTUBE WITH GALE
There's a Bear on a Bench
Throwing Rocks in the River

NON-FICTION
Caught in the Crosshairs of War

GALE'S FAMILY VIDEOS AVAILABLE ON LINE
Live! Little Stockey & the Miracle of Christmas

Animals & Music Volume 1
Animals & Music Volume 2
Animals & Music Volume 3
Animals & Music Volume 4
Animals & Music Volume 5

Made in the USA
Middletown, DE
01 March 2025

72044562R00024